ALI BABA AND THE FORTY THIEVES

ONCE UPON A TIME, THERE WAS A WOODCUTTER NAMED ALI BABA.

EVERY DAY, ALONG WITH HIS DONKEY, HE WOULD CLIMB THE MOUNTAIN TO GATHER FIREWOOD.

ONE DAY, WHILE HE STOPPED TO REST UNDER A TREE, HE HEARD SOME VOICES. WHEN HE LOOKED FOR WHERE THE SOUND WAS COMING FROM, HE SAW 40 MEN IN FRONT OF A ROCK.

SUDDENLY, ONE OF THEM UTTERED A MAGIC PHRASE, CAUSING THE STONE TO MOVE ASIDE AND REVEAL A SECRET CAVE.

AT THAT MOMENT, ALI BABA IMAGINED THAT THOSE MEN WERE BANDITS, BUT HE WANTED TO KNOW WHAT WAS INSIDE THE CAVE.

THEN, AS SOON AS THE 40 THIEVES LEFT, HE
STOOD IN FRONT OF THE CAVE AND REPEATED
THE PHRASE HE HEARD: 'OPEN, SESAME!'
THE STONE MOVED IMMEDIATELY, REVEALING
THE HIDDEN CAVE.

UPON ENTERING THE CAVE, ALI BABA ENCOUNTERED MANY JEWELS, SILVERWARE, GOLD COINS, AND CHESTS FULL OF TREASURE.

EXCITED ABOUT THE FORTUNE, HE TOOK EVERYTHING THAT WAS POSSIBLE TO CARRY ON HIS DONKEY'S BACK, COVERED IT WITH A LITTLE FIREWOOD, AND WENT HOME.

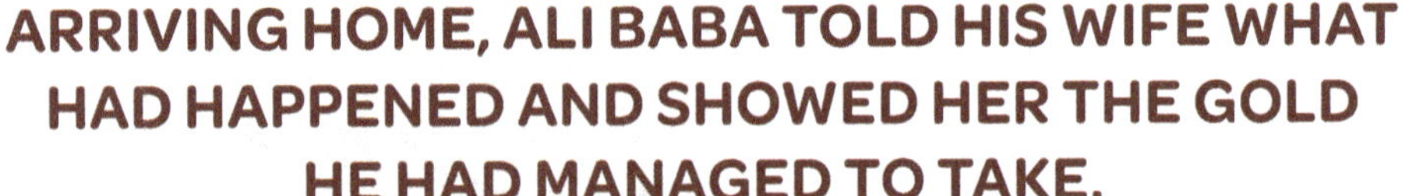

ARRIVING HOME, ALI BABA TOLD HIS WIFE WHAT
HAD HAPPENED AND SHOWED HER THE GOLD
HE HAD MANAGED TO TAKE.

THEN, HE ASKED HIS WIFE TO WEIGH THE
COINS AND THEN HIDE THE ENTIRE FORTUNE.

AFTER A FEW DAYS, ALI BABA LEARNED THAT THE SULTAN WAS SEARCHING FOR SOME THIEVES WHO HAD STOLEN ALL HIS TREASURE.

SUSPICIOUS THAT THOSE WERE THE MEN HE HAD SEEN, HE DECIDED TO TELL THE SULTAN THE WHOLE TRUTH. MEANWHILE, THE THIEVES CONTINUED TO STORE THE STOLEN OBJECTS IN THE SECRET CAVE.

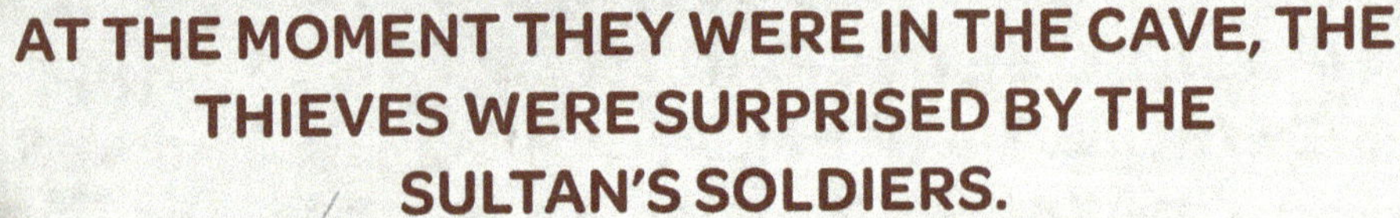
AT THE MOMENT THEY WERE IN THE CAVE, THE THIEVES WERE SURPRISED BY THE SULTAN'S SOLDIERS.

WITHOUT BEING ABLE TO ESCAPE, THEY WERE CAUGHT AND ARRESTED BY THE SOLDIERS. THE SULTAN, IN TURN, MANAGED TO RECOVER ALL HIS FORTUNE.

ALI BABA ALSO RETURNED ALL THE MONEY HE HAD TAKEN FROM THE CAVE, BUT THE SULTAN DECIDED TO REPAY HIS HONESTY BY PRESENTING HIM WITH MANY GOLD COINS.

THEN, ALI BABA AND HIS WIFE BECAME RICH
AND LIVED HAPPILY EVER AFTER.

The collection **Classic Tales - Once Upon a Time** reunites the most popular stories in children's literature. In each volume, a different narrative is presented simply and charmingly for the little readers.

In this edition, we retell the story of **Ali Baba and the Forty Thieves**, which tells the tale of a woodcutter who discovers the secret treasure of thieves who cross his path and sees his life take a new direction.

IBC – INSTITUTO BRASILEIRO DE CULTURA LTDA
CNPJ 04.207.648/0001-94
Avenida Juruá, 762 – Alphaville Industrial
ZIP CODE: 06455-907 – Barueri/SP
www.editoraonline.com.br

On line
EDITORA

Chair: Paulo Roberto Houch
MTB 0083982/SP

Editorial Coordination: Paola Houch
Writing: Mara Luongo
Visual Programmer (Intern): Raissa Ribeiro
Publisher: Leonardo Houch
Images: Shutterstock
Sales number: +55 (11) 3393-7723 (vendas@editoraonline.com.br)

ISBN 978-65-6126-079-4

9 786561 260794